This is Rachel Leadbetter's second written work to be published. She is a mother and a wife, leading a very busy life, working two jobs. Writing has been a lifelong passion for Rachel, originating as childhood stories crafted both as creative play and respite from the pains of rheumatoid arthritis. Though the condition never fully took hold, Rachel's drive to write persevered strictly for pleasure, until recently when she finally felt ready to bring her imaginative worlds to life. Bolstered by her proud husband and two grown children with families of their own, Rachel is thrilled to be sharing this latest labour of love.

Dedicated to Terry—much loved father, husband and Gramps. I did it, Dad.

Also, to my mum, a talented lady with spiritual insight—my best friend.

And last but not least, to Oscar—my absolute world.

I want to thank my husband who is always so supportive and proud. He helped me a lot with this particular book and even though he may not like horror he has a good imagination. Stu—always and forever XX.

"Student – Our self is our ego, is this our self-esteem, our integrity, What if we lost it?"

Master: "If we lost our ego, which could be our window to our self-esteem, then we could sink into depression and despair. Integrity would not be in question, as there would be no thought for others at this point."

Everything begins with a thought, yet nothing lasts…

What is 'IS' until it's GONE? Is that thought worth bargaining for?

"In everything that is ordinary, it is possible to glimpse the extraordinary from a shaft of sunlight to a star up above… if you really want to take that chance. Is it not easier to accept what you see and run with it…?" said the possible voice of reason.

Chapter 1

I opened my eyes and realised I was taking strong and firm strides across what appeared to be a desert. The heat was strong and dry. The air above the ground shimmered in a haze of heat, but I could feel nothing. My outer shell seemed warm but my inside was as cold as ice.

My name was Ramone. Of that I knew, a man who always seemed to have money, good rugged looks and very few words. Feelings didn't seem to register or matter, if indeed I had any. I was aware of travelling forwards to find a greater source, but I didn't understand why or care. I existed in the here and now and saw only highlights of the past, if relevant to the here and now in flashbacks. I only understood that everything would become clear the closer I got to the source, the infinite, the power and the reason for my existence.

The start of the end:

As I entered the quiet little town of Lakebridge, a wind kicked up, buffering my long black leather coat around my calves as if in a reliable, reassuring welcome. I strode purposefully towards the saloon bar and ordered my drink—whiskey and ice. I gave the bar man a drink too to keep him happy. I was immediately approached by one of the local fun ladies—short, bubbly, longish brown hair, ample chest around a cheeky Size 14/16. Enough for me to get my claws into, no pun intended. My conversation was short and meaningful. She giggled as she walked, jostling her ample breasts about, knowing she was in for a good screwing (as an appetizer anyway). The boobs were her power and her sexy gait with her genitals added to this efficacy of self-power. Little did the useless tart know it was her last screw and I was going to suck the life source out of her throbbing and easily given veins... I followed her up the stairs, struck by her confidence and amiable gait.

I left little mess. I was always a clean diner, and as I came back into the bar again after shutting the bedroom door, I carefully and quickly eyed up my next victim. Sex didn't matter; to me, the end result was always the same. I decided the waitress with the more ample bosom was the next meal ticket. All I did was whisper 'I need you' in her ear and she instantly followed me upstairs. My earlier meal was under the bed, carefully covered with a blanket.

As usual, my lady satisfied me, going straight for my genitals. As I ejaculated into her waiting mouth, I sank my teeth into her throbbing temples and drew out bits of brain, tissue and lots of life blood. My fingernails cut open her carotid artery and I drank eagerly. My lady had no time to squeal; I was quick and caring. After all, she did seem to like me...

I knew after a while someone would come and check on us to see if we were OK. Bar and whorehouse it may be, but clients were checked to see if they paid up. I tore out my first lady's heart and chewed on it as I carefully tidied up the room. I understood these whores had families and friends and my learnt empathy would want them to find their deceased in an understandable decent state of affairs. As I heard footsteps approaching, I exited through a side window, slightly aware of my nails catching the ground and a feeling of freedom but a need to camouflage myself. I headed over to some grassland. I stood up, slowly feeling my body shape changing, panting and hot. My eyes adjusted to the dark and I noticed my paws were in pouncing mode. I lay in wait.

I heard people shouting and screaming and someone saying it was the Devil in human form. Shots were fired into the darkness as if to scare me away. Guns did not frighten me. Only a silver bullet would do some damage or an extremely religious man of God. I had ate one once. He was rather chewy and a bit bitter, not an enjoyable meal at all. Humans are very fickle; they can be Catholics one minute, but if the deal seems more prosperous, say on the Protestant side, then they'll just swap and convince themselves that God supports their decision. After all, isn't 'God' so forgiving, loving and understanding? He's also easily desert-able and relatively boring. He created life. He gave them a fickle heart and low intelligence and an ability to see and understand only that they see, believe in only that they themselves can see and believe in only what is evident. Humans were given choice and use it as they do to follow like sheep—silly fuckin' sheep! I do question the actions of the universe sometimes as if someone at the time was having a laugh.

Hence, my life was easy. What people didn't understand, they ran away from… Sex, money and the power of the mind was enough to bring people close to me. A meal was always just around the corner. My meal was always on my mind among other things. This was my survival mode.

I stood up slowly feeling my body shape changing and I soon felt my coat flapping against my calves and knew my shape was acceptable. I drifted round to the dwellings far enough away from the bar and decided to settle at the one with the chubby-cheeked woman inside.

As I knocked the door, I felt at ease and also a little saddened and knew that being a good listener in this home would secure me some time to recuperate and maybe socialise before my next feed. I kinda felt I needed some attention and acceptance to me, to what they saw and to what they felt on seeing me. The door opened and my host-to-be smiled and allowed my entry. The home, though small, was friendly and comfortable, with a roaring fire and a pot of stew on top of it. The whole of the inside was like many others I had visited, open plan and untidily welcome. My rather fat host was named Sarah Jayne but said I could call her SJ for short. I introduced myself as Joseph John (as I liked to ridicule the Bible apostles) but allowed her to call me JJ.

I described myself as a traveller trying to find myself (What a fuckin laugh!) She loved this!!! She wanted to be my saviour of lost souls. I listened to her life story and accepted tea and stew from her. I found out her children's names—Sophie, Marcus and Robert. They were friendly, inquisitive and so, so innocent. I made a decision when I met the children as they had such an effect on me. I decided to leave this family in peace and not burden them with grief and heartache. When Robert senior returned home, he was amicable, though very tired after his day's work at the foundry. He gave me some blankets and helped me make a makeshift bed up by the fire. I confided in him that I would be leaving at first light and gave him a black velvet purse full of five gold coins.

Robert Senior made a fuss of not being able to accept such treasures and I admired his simple pride. He had very little to his name and I knew the coins would make a huge difference to his quality of life and set his family up. We drank some homebrewed ale and then settled to sleep. As I woke early as usual, I quietly left the dwelling to stretch my legs. During my stretch, I came across a wild pig which I gutted and took back to the family. I left the coins and the pig as a thank-you gift.

Leaving the dwelling as quietly as I approached it, I felt saddened to some extent. The family life was something I liked the look of. Everyone seemed content and comfortable. I guess that was what happiness was for some people. I was unable to remain in one spot for long due to hiding my identity. I risked my life every time I showed myself to other species. Humans were fickle and easy to manipulate, but every so often, I came across a shapeshifter, demon or vampire, and I then had to face a very different battle.

Alternate realm species (which is what I liked to call every part-living dead thing that doesn't normally and shouldn't walk on the earth) can be very territorial with not only their 'family' (chosen human family) but also their town or village etc. This also complicated the situation when the species chose to inhabit a human host. Clearly, the host to all humans around is totally accepted as the body or shell is recognised as Aunt Sally (for example). However, unbeknown to the humans, their aunt is effectively dying. Once her soul has been completely overridden and consumed by the species, then the body itself begins to die. The species then has to take over another host as quickly as possible. This process can take up to 10 years and more if the body can be treated well, so the humans have already welcomed the species into their lives, hence the emotional attachment. This process is although quite debilitating to the human, providing stress and grief as part of the cycle, but also provides security and protection for the species.

It was important for certain species to be accepted to maintain equilibrium and the possibility of reproducing. If a species can settle somewhere and live comfortably under the human guise, that's all that can be expected. There was a lot about inhumans, shapeshifters that mankind was not familiar with, but I had my serious doubts that everyone was oblivious.

My journey from the quaint dwelling was an uneventful one. I travelled by day in my human form and continued the nightly pace in my animal form, hunting for food and pleasure and getting sleep as and when needed. My journey stopped again when I reached a town called Coyote Ranch. I approached in my human form but as a female. I dressed myself in jeans, walking boots, a khaki jumper and a jacket-type raincoat. I gave myself jet-black long hair which I tied in the nape of my neck. I wore some costume jewellery comprising a gold cross on a gold necklace, small but noticeable, gold-stud earrings and a gold ring on the insignificant hand signalling my nonmarital status. I had a backpack with me and I stored some of my personal things in there, instead of keeping it in my nuclear realm (my words for my safe place in my alternate dimension).

Chapter 2

I entered a coffee-type shop and was soon sat with a strong latte and a ham and cheese toastie. (Strange how to blend in, I easily called upon my other digestive system to deal with processed crap.) I struck up a conversation with the manager (who I found out was the owner too and highly educated on current town affairs). She was a friendly person clinging on the edge of about 67, pleasant, chatty and very welcoming. We talked about the town that I was passing through but hoped to stay a while, maybe. I left it uncertain and allowed her to draw her own conclusions about that. Barbara (nice name, and she said it with a drawl *Barrrrrbarrrrarrr.*) recommended her Bed and Breakfast place. This sounded amazing, and I jumped at the chance. The opportunity of a lifetime seemed to be casually entering my realm, a chance to remain somewhere, to feel a part of something, someone or somewhere to actually belong if I could be granted such a luxury. If this was what my journey was all about, then maybe I could settle for a while.

Barbara asked the young assistant to take over, and she walked me to the B an B, chatting aimlessly about the town and the people in it. Upon reaching the quaint red-bricked building, I felt a comfort settle over me. I took this chance to let my guard down and make contacts. Barb (as she wanted to be called) found out I was 28, possibly escaping an abusive boyfriend, orphaned as a young child and in need of settling down and being happy. I would be looking to secure a job to pay my way and for somewhere more permanent hopefully. Barb gave me a key to the front door, told me the guestrooms were made up and I could choose which one I preferred, telling me tea was at six and left me to my own devices.

My story was clearly believable and I got the feeling Barb had come to the rescue of many young ladies in distress before. The property was spacious with two reception rooms downstairs and four big bedrooms on the second floor. The décor was a mixture of creams and light greens which blended well with wooden floors and panelling to the walls. I chose my room swiftly by the view the windows offered. I didn't want to be overlooking the street but preferred the very neat, busy and manicured garden at the back of the house. I chose fresh flowers out of the garden and arranged them in some vases out of the kitchen and placed them around the house. I felt this quite feminine touch was a nice example of me wanting to feel at home and embracing my female shell. The house was so tidy and very clean. Barb was a clean freak and clearly enjoyed being this way.

I soon began to really establish myself and made a point of being everywhere but nowhere for long. I smiled and acknowledged people, continuing with my new role in the shop. I was the helpful one, always polite and keen to serve, and I worked hard. To the town folk, I was an enigma. I didn't seem to have a bad day and I was always quietly happy. I looked good and I smelt good all the time. I noticed my assistant was a bit sweaty around the moist areas of the torso, and I reminded myself to always make sure I was smelling appealing. Sweat wasn't something I did but I excreted moisture when happy and that was something I would always try to pop to the loo to get rid of. No one ever noticed. To Barb, I was the perfect employee. I never complained, always worked hard and covered shifts when Sally was poorly or drunk from the night before. I never said 'no' to Barb and I made sure when I cleaned up the shop, at the end of a shift, the floor was clean enough to eat off. Sally was a good time girl and wasn't particular about her appearance at times. However, she was lovely and had a good personality which made up for the lack of body-conscious incidents.

I did have to be careful at times, as I was something too good to be true, and I had to make simple mistakes to prove I was real. I could pick up around 280 kilos in weight without exerting myself, and sometimes I did forget that a human woman is not supposed to do this. My speed for getting things completed was also too fast, so unless I was alone, I had to remember to slow down. I mirrored others and learnt a lot from watching. Human behaviour is quite sexual; it's like watching the mating routines of a peacock. The male makes sure he is seen from all angles and preens himself constantly. He's checking out the area and the quality of the female. He changes all his behaviours to appear desirable to the one he has chosen to impress. However, with humans, they appear to want to impress the crowd around the person they want, and opinions appear to really matter.

If anyone comes in the way of the male, he appears to change tactics and become like a praying mantis to protect his chosen one. This perception of mate then being seen as trophy, then food, was quite an awesome thought to me. In this respect, humans were not that different from myself at all. Dependent on the age of the onlooker, the ritual was viewed very differently. It appeared the older you were, the sight of someone being preen like and showing off resulted in them being a cock and needing to grow up. For a female, she was seen as easy, a bit of a tart. In my realm, what was, was. There is no definite way to behave unless you were with an elder. Gender was irrelevant as any shapeshifter can procreate and the reasons behind doing it were to carry on with the species and any off/half/part-breed was seen as adventurous. Each realm had their own hierarchy and so-called rules to abide by. This was seen as minimal obedience to keep utter control. There was no need for any written law or members of a cabinet or any officiates like police, as what was, was. United we would be if attack was foreseen. Survival and longevity of race was what was important. Not a particular one specie, but only one needed to be left standing. Opinions and feelings were overrated and exhausting. And I found that by following a careful programme of pretence.

Was it hard being a female in other people's eyes…? For them, no, but for me, yes. The urge to change, to clone, to shift was incompressible at points. I was in effect an outcast but an accepted, unknown and not-understood outsider. Sometimes I felt as if I had on strong, thick tights which pressed against me in all the delicate areas, restricting my movements. This feeling did get on top of me at times.

My life had challenges, but then I found more arrived. People around me grew up, got older, got sick, had dental problems and gave blood etc. I didn't do any of these things. I remained the same constantly. God forbid, if there was an epidemic, I would stand out like a sore thumb. My outer shell would age differently if I took over a being, but I was using my shift to stay a female and enter the human population.

I got to know a lot of people of all ages. I got to be a part of a group of peers who all wanted to be sociable and have a drink every now and then. I was placed in a book club with a library group all women (Barb's idea). I also joined the athletics club at the local gym so I could get some running in. What with work and my newfound social life, I was so busy; I didn't have time to be creative with myself, so I remained the same way all the time, every time. The running gave me an outlet of sorts. I could part-shift as I ran if I was by myself. I would just churn up the inner layer a bit to expand the outer. The human naked eye would never see this, but for me, it was the ultimate relief. The book club, well, let's say it was as boring as a person playing solo snap! However, for me, it was a chance to blend in, which was important if I decided to stay around. Blend in and not stand out was the effect I was after.

I ate well. Barb was a good cook and made sure I was fed. Her food was really good and there was lots of it. She seemed to really have some feelings for me, and this was welcomed. When I worked the late shift, she always had something ready made for me and it was freshly cooked or prepared.

The running club had a two-day run booked in the neighbouring county where I was asked to take part. I allegedly had good stamina. This was exciting, a two-day trip and lots of fun. I said I would love to go and looked forward to it. For me, this was what I needed, to get out without doing anything odd or unexpected. I could still blend in, take part and escape at some point hopefully. We discussed the route and who was taking who, etc. We talked about who was sleeping where, and it was decided and plans were made.

Everyone was excited. They took the challenge very seriously and there was healthy competition with the other county.

I slept a restless night as I had started to experience what I would call leg cramps. I felt maybe this was due to being in one form all the time. I dare not shift, as there was always someone near to me at any one time. I could shift swiftly, but it was a risk. Even during the night, I felt I could be watched or someone would just burst through the door. There was always one room used for guests at least, so the house was always full of life at any one time.

I desperately wanted to shift to lose the skin which felt like an elastic band at times, cutting the air out of me and preventing me from moving. My head swam with ideas, but I knew I couldn't act out any of them safely, without giving away my destination and my identity. I needed to change my diet and quick. I knew what I needed and how to get it—just needed to make sure I acquired it soon.

We set off together as a team, with enough packed in a bag to last us for the two days and one night. Barb had also made us some packed lunches and this came in handy. It was around a 3.5-hour journey. Conversation was light and daft, and time went fast. We chatted about past partners and conquests and I joined in to a point, remaining a little vague, not wanting to give too much away. We arrived and got ourselves set up in an inn. Three to a room, stuff on the beds and, as a group, we went into the bar. We were meeting tomorrow at 10 for the run. This included breakfast at eight and then the meetup. We were with another two local teams for fun races. So that meant the plan for tonight was drinks at the bar, and this was happy time. Alcohol was never an issue for me, as I absorbed it and had no effect. However, I had to fake this to fit in. I had seen plenty of pissed humans in my short period of time in this realm. Everyone differed in their reactions to alcohol. Some got very happy, almost as if they couldn't be happy without it. Some got loud and silly. Some acted like they had the devil inside of them. Some even cried nonstop. There was a period of time where they all showed signs of euphoria before this. I bided my time, watching everyone knock drinks back. They got louder and stupider each time. I danced around a bit like they did, raising my glass into the air. There were only a few of us left in the bar and when I had accounted for everyone and felt sure, they all knew and accepted I was there. (As being there was normal, I was the quiet but present, one that was there but not there, heard but not heard and seen but not seen.) I slipped away quietly.

I walked out until I came to the edge of the forest around the corner from the inn. Once on the grass, I crouched down in the dark. Slowly, I unfolded and let my skin loosen up and fall away into the atmosphere. There would be no sign of this, nothing to suggest I had even been there. I felt myself stretch and roll. The feeling is like no other, like an orgasmic feeling with relief, freedom and full self-worth. I lay on the ground on my back and then suddenly jumped onto my feet, all four of them. Feeling the undergrowth between my claws, I gripped the ground tighter and sped off. I felt the creature I had chosen take over and lead me to freedom and food. I ate some live appetisers on the way and stole their life source and drank their blood. I ran and ran and ran until I then changed form again. I didn't know what I had become straight away, but I felt the freedom of lift. I fluttered wings and aimed higher. It was times like this that I was able to let myself do what it chose to do. I had switched from *canis lupus* to *numquid avis tincta* (bird of prey). My newfound raptor sense was ready for food and to exercise its senses and take by force. I scanned the ground, looking and sensing motion. It only took the slightest second for me to see and feel its presence. I swooped down to secure my prey when I was suddenly alerted to a much larger movement to my right.

I sensed a human, and it was totally pickled. Other than that, generally well, no cancers, no recent illness, just a sadness but nothing lingering. I flew overhead and he didn't notice or hear me. I sat on his shoulder and then he noticed me. He looked closely at me, and when he bent his head in further, I popped his eye out. Sinking my beak into the soft tissue through the iris and into the lens, I sucked the vitreous fluid before frantically gouging the pupil out with the optic nerve included. I swallowed this whole. The human fell onto the floor and I sank my beak into the pulsing carotid to suck the life force out. The feeling, the satisfaction, was enormous. I changed shape and ran like a cougar back to the edge of the green. As I dropped down to the floor, I felt my shape change again and I had the snug fit feeling around my body again. I stood up and made my way back into the bar area where everyone was singing at this time.

No one knew I had been missing—it was like I hadn't been away. This is how it always worked unless I met up with one of mine. I am hard to predict, hard to keep track of and hard to fathom. We went to our rooms and I staggered up in the same way they did. We climbed into beds and my two roommates were out almost straight away. I lay there for a while, listening to the deep breathing and then evolving into guttural drunken snoring. Neither of them moved much. So intoxicated, I did wonder how any of them would be running tomorrow.

I was one of the first awake in our room. Breakfast was a full English served at 8:30 a.m. I took on the role of calling everyone and getting them all sat around the table. This was a complicated affair, but we managed it. The exercise, the running and the games were really good. I actually had lots of fun! It was very competitive, and again I had to remind myself that winning everything is not always humanly possible. We decided to remain one more night. I settled again for the evening in the bar. There was live entertainment with some dancers and a singer. I didn't want to take my chances going out again. I was lucky last night—very lucky. There was an opportunity to join in with the singing, and we all had a go. I even surprised myself—with no magic used, I actually had a good voice. The night ran smoothly. The next day loomed as we packed our things and got ready for the drive home. I sensed something off, and I could feel a draining energy. My friends were low, as recovering from the alcohol but there was something else. We drove back to the town and settled back into routine and continued with our lives.

I was at the café the next day when I was approached by a man in a dark suit. He strode up to the counter asking for a black coffee. I served him and he stared at me, right into my soul. He had a book with him, which he made a show of writing notes in. To all around, he was an outsider visiting for coffee before going back on his way. To me, he was communicating with me while I was serving and being the 'me' that was expected. Customers left and I ended my shift by cleaning. The man at the table, only then seen by me, became apparent. This was 'ME', the 'me' in the other realm.

The 'me' that was there to warn me that I must move again; I must start up again. I was being chased by something far more powerful than anyone could imagine. My quest for the ultimate power had to continue and my little drift off that path to experience acceptance was making it all too hard for fate to continue down its designated path.

I had made no close relationships, no major bonds with anyone and I hadn't killed anyone in the town. However, being here had caused a rolling effect like a domino. I had infected the town with my presence. I had made myself fit in and had forged bonds within the close community. I had fucked up. It all had to go. I didn't know I was being tracked until my other self came to tell me. Obviously, the goal of the power, the force we are all drawn to, is being sought by others as well. My little holiday had placed all these people in danger. The others that would come looking would not be pleasant. They didn't care about fitting in; they weren't bothered about being invisible, and they just wanted to reach the goal by any means necessary and fuck whatever was in their path.

I had to vacate without leaving any of me behind. I had impacted on memory, but I definitely had no love interests that I knew of.

So decision made, I had to move…

Chapter 3

Finishings and to new beginnings…

Memory is what is seen and felt and therefore is believable. So if it's possible to reinvent memory, then the seeing and feeling can be remodelled. If I'm there but I'm not there, what part of me is actually there? I've been entering people's realms and disturbing their harmonious lives for a long time now. Yes, I can alter fate in that respect and I can hold all the cards but I had to keep deliberate interferences undercover to some extent. I decided that the only way for me to disappear with a believable story was to become my own victim. They would then add this to the body that was found a couple of nights ago, and it would become clear a serial killer was on the loose and they couldn't say that much about me, as I only told them what they needed to know, and with memory fading in humans, little is left of complete fact.

I didn't want to upset Barb, but she was the one that would find me. I cloned myself and made sure I looked tired. I walked past Barb and her group while she was watching the hands of the card players on show, saying I was popping out for some air. She said, "Be careful," absently as she was engrossed in her game. A win at this point for Barb would make her a key player and keep her at the top of her game. I felt a little sorry for her, as she had been so good to me.

I set off through town and made my way to the edge where the wilderness began. This was my place to be found and I had already placed the memory in Barbara's head, so she would think in the next hour or so to come looking for me. I decided I needed to mirror my kill the other night so officers could determine we had both been killed by the same killer. As I stepped out of myself, I looked carefully, checking that all parts looked credible. I pooped my one eye out and chucked it on the side. I pierced the carotid and drained the copycat carcass of fluid. To the human eye, I looked like I had been attacked quite viciously, lost an eye and suffered from pernicious anaemia through force. I took a last look at the scene under my feet and the scene in front of me. The town which had accommodated and made me feel welcomed and safe was now to become a memory for as long as I wanted it to remain. I wasn't sentimental and I certainly didn't feel a necessary longing for a partner, but I did have some thoughts of regret of leaving. I slowly turned away and changed my position to take on my new form. As I left the ground flexing my knees and feeling the air under my feet, I spread my wings and fluttered the ends of the feathers, stretching myself inward and outwardly to take on the new form in an adequate way and to avoid detection from others.

I flew and flew over more land and sea and kept going and going until I reached a point of tiredness and had to fly down to the ground to rest. In the form of a snake, I crawled under a large stone and slept fitfully. My sleep was pursued with dreams of what I had left behind and what could have been.

Above everything, my eagerness for food and my quest prevailed.

As the sun began to rise, I snuck out behind my rock and hunted. I hunted for the need to eat the need to survive and thrive. As I sucked and chewed the unwilling meats of rodents and insects, I realised I really thrived on the thrill, and so I sought to move onwards to complete this. I started to flap out my wings and stretch my claws and I took flight, covering large expanses of land and reaching forward.

Life and death is what it is all about—death dances silently in everyone's shadow and she doesn't give a damn. Why else would I surround myself with mortals... to avoid the agony of loss? To them, a loss is an abyss and nothing fills that space. I can gain an energy from the negative that consumes some beings. I didn't understand myself totally, didn't like myself half the time, but I liked being something else and boredom can't set in when it's so transient.

Feeling the constant pull like a magnet, I carried on ploughing through towns, villages, different terrains and seeing lots of different life. The hours turned into days and then into weeks. My forms shifted throughout my journeys and I was careful to always choose carefully. Wouldn't want to fall prey to a more sinister creature while I was in play mode. Being in half shift would make me extremely vulnerable.

I came upon a little village in the desert plains. I felt a tug here to remain for a while. I decided my male form would suffice here. A middle-aged man with a slight limp—a plausible story and just distinguished enough to be noticeable but not too noticeable or it could be seen as a threat. I approached a bar and started minimal conversation whilst ordering a whiskey. They were short on staff and needed someone to work the evening shifts due to a vacancy. When I enquired why the vacancy was there, I was told the kid was shot due to philandering with other people's women. I showed how shocked I was and said I wasn't about to get myself shot, but if the job was available, I was in.

Chapter 4

Fast shift forward two months, and I'm in the upstairs flat having my tool sucked the life out of by Frannie, who I had been seeing the past two weeks. Frannie was fun, sweet and innocent-looking but rode me like a bull on heat! She had been hurt by men previously and was shy when I met her but had definitely improved in my two weeks of contact. It felt nice to be liked again and I had missed the humanly touch. My skin covering was happy and chilled, and I enjoyed the testosterone feeling I was left with once Frannie had finished with me. We were a couple; how bizarre was that?

I had made some friends and stopped a few fights, drank way too much beer and all appeared to be going very well. Then the shit hit the fan... Friday evening visitors, no one knew, walking into the saloon with an air of purpose, six of them, each with a sexy, rugged look but unholy as hell. Jason, our manager, asked what drinks they wanted and welcomed them to the saloon, making small one-sided conversation. The men were threatening in their outlook and held an air of greatness. I knew they were one to watch and I had to act. Very popular with the ladies, these men were something of an enigma. I watched them flaunt themselves as they socialised and they knew they were admired.

I remained quiet, did what I had to and stayed in the background but maintained a good view. I managed to get some time that evening to cut the shift, so I got into action. The external door was by the toilets and washrooms. I placed myself by the door with a cigarette and let my blonde hair fall carelessly over my right shoulder. I was covered up but showed some neck, just enough to let the mind do some creative imagining. I heard the middle door open and recognised the sharp smell of subspecies. I worked my cloak of masking energies and smiled absently as I walked away towards one of the cars in the parking lot, knowing he had already seen me. As I turned round the corner, I crouched between two vehicles and let myself feel catlike. As he approached the gap in the cars, I jumped up and carved out his heart from his chest with my elongated claws. He didn't stand a chance, and I watched the body disappear to ash. I knew I had to work quickly to remove any trace and then start on the remaining ones. The fact that alternate species were sharing the same realm as myself was evidence enough that there was a rush to get to the ONE, whoever and whatever that was. I had to eliminate my competition quickly and cleanly.

Two more appeared by the door, making their way through the car park, their hasty approach kicking the dust up through the dimly lit area. Their appearances changed and they became a mixture of fluidity, jelly and half-formed mammal. Their ability to change with speed was not practised and I had no issue to finish each one off. I drove my fist through the heart of the one, and whilst eating the extremely warm and pulsing organ, I put my foot through the fluid brain-like tissue before stomping down hard, then locating the heart which I left behind the wheel of the car. As I watched both forms dissolve into ash, I squeezed the torn heart between my fingers and dribbled enough here and there whilst I crossed the road and made off into the desert. It wasn't long when the sound of movement allowed me warning of their approach. It was a flurry of wings and feet but at a speed, so no wariness involved, just pure unholy killing on its mind. I remained in my tree, hidden by foliage. Although sparse, I was camouflaged. I felt the wings caress my area and I reached out a sharp tentacle, piercing with total accuracy the heart of the form. Like a trocar, I not only pierced the object while suspending it midair but also drained it at the same time. As I felt the liquid being sucked through my own made cannula into my own form, I continued until all nonhuman life was left. Like a dried up prune, I let the form go and allowed it to dissipate into the air like dust. So eventually, all that was left was a fine mist, no particles of solid matter, just a memory of what was held in the finest particles of water now being dried up within seconds.

I slowly moved position to another part of the terrain, and this time, I was floor level. As my shape changed, I felt a little vulnerable but also knew I was practically undetectable. As a scarab beetle, I lay quiet and in wait. Sounds of paws, then footfalls, then wings, then indiscernible screams. I felt the proximity stir my otherwise hidden needs only noticeable when in that particular form, of wanting to devour human flesh. Being so small, you would think I would feel vulnerable and scared. However, I felt a sense of power. I sensed movement as something ran past, then slowed and then stopped. I scrambled up to the form and snuck in through the plantar arch of the foot, making my way through the trajectory of metatarsal veins until I was at the base of the ankle. There,

I struck up a bond with the dorsalis pedis and followed up to the fibular, tibia and then rested at the femoral. Here I sat and dug down deep to ingest liquid and life force. I drained and drained until all was gone. All shapeshifted organs were drained and life force from the arterial blood gorged on. Poof, the remaining carcass desperately trying to shift from shape to shape but unable to do so completely due to the excess of fluid loss slowly crumbled into dust as it gave up the will to carry on. I rolled over, recoiling from the surge of ingested fluids and I let my shape change to that of a scorpion. I crawled into the terrain and remained quiet. Feeling a little bit sick, I stored some ingested fluids in my parallel universe to prevent me from slowing down. There was nothing happening around me, no sound. Everything was a very eerie stillness. That's when I levitated as a fly and saw the familiar signs of the swirl of sand and wind reminiscent of a small tornado commonly known as a rope. This would be the sign of one being, entering or leaving a realm. If more beings travelled in this way, the swirl would be bigger in appearance like a cyclone. Often, weather type of events were a common form of travel and accepted by humans as a natural phenomenon. This swirl told me one had got away before I could stop him. He would be able to confirm my existence in this part of the plain and my actions towards his kind. As the tornado left, I formed back into the man known at the inn and I appeared in the bar area again, carrying on with my shift.

That night, I lay in bed thinking about events and planning my next steps. I could dissipate into my realm and appear somewhere else, but I wouldn't know what I had missed. Signs to be seen are not always visible when in a realm, and the energy needed to realm hop would be huge in comparison from moving and shifting towards my goal. The pull was still there and its power was even stronger, so I had a trajectory still, and I needed to make tracks.

Decision made—I left, first thing, leaving a note to explain my move. I said I felt homesick and needed to see my old family/friends. I had never really discussed anything personal about me with anyone, so anything I said would be plausible. I made the bar presentable for the lunchtime shift and tidied my room completely, removing all signs of my existence. I took a bottle of whiskey as payment for my last few shifts and explained this in the note. I left in my preferred form of an eagle and started my journey again. As I travelled, I thought of Frannie and how tentative she was towards me. This would be missed, and for the briefest of moments, I felt some sorrow for her pain to come with my sudden absence. She had no faith in men and I just secured that unfaith by leaving her in the lurch after a two-week fling with passion… Oh, well. Moment gone, onwards and onwards now for me.

Chapter 5

Over terrain, over life I flew, capturing it all in a heartbeat. Everything below me had a story from the crustaceous earth to the crawling insect, from the tiniest lizard to the human being. Everything had a past and a present; not all had a future. I was part of the reason for the lack of future in some cases but all with good reason—a defensive tactic, a survival tactic, a passionate tactic, a stay-alive tactic. I didn't usually toy with my food but I did take every opportunity to enjoy it.

As I swept across skies in mid-storm, I never failed to take in the wonders of the natural world. I was also amazed by the alternative realms and the creativeness that actually made it all possible. I had many unanswered questions, but I totally felt the lack of need to know any information and I was happy to continue on, forever long my light stayed lit in the absence of such information. Travelling fast and slow, the element of time all but a mere myth, as I failed to realise the amount of time spent in transit in another form. My birdlike form felt free and I was safe to daydream, but it was also dangerous, as I wasn't alert. I knew I would be landing soon and eating to gain more strength for the road ahead. I decided to land near a little train station attached to quite a large town, a very busy town by all accounts. The station was full with lots of different people, countless deliveries of food and drink and everyone on a mission.

I morphed into a young man of about 19, fresh-faced but ruddy complexion, hands that were large and rough from lots of outside work. Dressed as a farmhand, I blended in well. I had the face of someone you knew and didn't bother speaking to. I looked an in-between type of 'He can cope but wouldn't it be good to mother him.' With men, I was suitably ignored, and with older women, I was looked upon caringly.

I had had many years of perfecting moulds and the suitability of them, given the purpose. Today, I was passing through gathering some drinks and food as I went. I passed the bar when a man asked me if I would be kind enough to help him with some lifting. He seemed pleasant enough and I got to work, carrying out his instructions. I had assembled all 12 of the barrels, ready for him to connect for the customers that very day. I also cleaned up the small cellar and helped myself to some cold beer while I waited for the next job. Old man Burt was thankful and shocked at the speed of my work and invited me for some food. He was a busy man at work, as well as having a large family. His wife, Belinda, was fierce in looks, with long, red hair and an ample frame with a sweet smile. The children were all aged from 12 months to 12 years, two girls and a boy. This was a busy family indeed.

Burt's staff came in to set up the bar, an array of large muscular men and very round busty ladies. I knew the type well, recognised their positives and negatives and saw their desires. I kept myself to myself, which was hard when people were intrigued. I managed that evening doing the odd jobs and Burt gave me the barn, advising me to lock the doors to keep in the horses. I got the feeling he was trying to say, to keep me safe. That night passed pleasantly enough. What with the general gurgle of the horses and the clippity-clop as they became restless at times, it was definitely quite serene. The next day was a warm setting with hardly any clouds. A spring in my pretend step, I made my way to the bar entrance where Belinda greeted me with a smile, showed me the restrooms and told me to make my way to the kitchen area for breakfast.

The sight that met me as I entered the kitchen would melt a normal person's human heart and soul, bringing about a number of emotions threatening to cascade tears of joy down a face. Of course in the absence of both a human heart and soul, in fact anything vaguely human, I recognised the need to relate to the picture I was met with and adjusted myself to find the appropriate actions and responses needed to suit and fit in perfectly. Kids were everywhere, looking cute, all smiley and happy, food around their lips and on their chins, little vests covered in sauce from the fresh sausage and bacon. All of them were looking at me with wonder and excitement, some of them doing that dribble thing when food and saliva dropped onto their chests.

I took my cap off and smiled long and hard, making my eyes twinkle. "What beautiful children you have and how happy they all are," I stated.

Belinda signalled me to sit. "They're lovely when they're borrowed." She narrowed her eyes and then started to laugh. "But I love 'em all," she said ecstatically.

Belinda was a raw, honest and loving woman and she gave me the impression that she would kill for her kids. Her love for her kin had no bounds, and this ignited me. This show of warmth and protection I felt was rare in the worlds I passed through. It gave me a warm tingle—quite unexpected. I felt I was in the presence of some real power.

I was soon sat at the table, listening to all stories about the farm, about the kids and what naughties they got up to while I stuffed myself with freshly cooked biscuits, sausage, bacon and fresh eggs. Surprisingly very hungry, I scoffed and scoffed until the plate was clean. After the second serving, I sat back and surveyed my buffet. Perfectly formed humans were all around me. It really was a pleasure to be fed by my food but I needed to do what I had to do before moving on. I planned for this evening to decease my newfound family and move on into the night.

The day passed pleasantly enough. I got a lot of jobs completed for Burt, and we had a jolly time whilst working. I actually liked the man a little. He was a hard working human with mouths to feed. But he was too trusting in every way. His staff wanted paying before the end of the month, so he did it. He gave some drinks away to some folk he knew well: 'It's on the house.' A hard working man, a loyal wife and crazy kids. He was a lot of fun to be around. I could see what his wife saw in him. He could sell ice to an Eskimo; this was how good his banter was.

Belinda prepped some food for the bar and kept the children busy at the same time. They followed instructions to the latter and performed their individual tasks well. If one wasn't aware of Burt's existence, one would assume Belinda was the landlady. She worked the lunch shift well and Burt took over for the evening. This was pure mom and babies' time then, which Belinda again excelled at. That evening was busy, with the 12-year-old having an issue with a local lad. As I helped behind the bar, I tuned in to the conversation upstairs.

Lyla (the 12-year-old) had been friendly with a 14-year-old called Robbie. He was a known prankster, a bit of a lad and a bit of a talker. He bragged about who he had kissed and made it known he had kissed Lyla. This, of course, pleased Belinda to no end. She had gleaned this information from the bakery staff. They had made their usual judgements and branded Lyla a hussy. Voices were raised as tensions grew. I turned up the volume of the country music downstairs to muffle the conversation. Burt threw me a grateful look and we continued with the shift. This must be killing Burt, him hearing some of this but not being able to respond to it.

I heard Lyla crying, saying she had trusted Robbie and thought he was the one for her. She had let him kiss her and touch her breast through the fabric, but she stopped him when he tried to get underneath her clothes. They had tussled and it got nasty, with him trying to force himself on her. He said he had done it before and there was nothing to worry about. He had scared her and she had shown Mom her arm where he had grabbed her, digging his nails into her flesh. It was at this point that the shouting stopped and the tears began. I could hear everything in detail, just as if I were in the room with them, but to a human, it was vague. The fact that the shouting had stopped alerted Burt—that things were calming down. I beckoned for Burt to pop upstairs to check on his family and I would cover the bar. He disappeared gratefully. I actually felt very human and very protective towards my new family. These were feelings I wasn't used to experiencing. My thoughts ceased when I heard a voice directly in front of me.

"Hey, newbie. What's your name?" said this woman of about 35, covered in makeup and wearing quite revealing clothes.

I studied her face, lines upon lines, coated quite thick with cream and powder. She had a detached soul, which meant to me she wasn't what she seemed. There was a nastiness to her, a two faced type of horrible and a used up sort of rag appearance.

"It's Jason, ma'am, and I'm just here for a brief while."

"How about we make it a longer while? I am very good with helping people feel at home and relaxed…" Makeup face did this thing with her eyelashes which resembled a type of seizure (to me). I stifled a laugh.

"I really am feeling quite homely enough. Thank you, ma'am. Now do you want a drink?" I pointed to all what was on offer.

"You really don't know what you're missing," she whispered, getting close to my ear, the breath quite rancid and her tongue dangerously close to my lobe. "Most men come around eventually when they see what's really on offer, even Burt every now and then…" She put her finger to her lips, making a shushing sound as she stepped back to look into my eyes.

I leant into her neck, breathing slow, and whispered to her. Suddenly, she stood upright and walked stiffly out the bar, ignoring the taunts from the regulars. One shouted, "Yes, Eve, now stop out. No one wants your used up ass here."

"Wow!" Burt said from the side of the bar. "What did you say to her to make her leave so suddenly? She always lingers in here, drinking herself stupid until someone takes her home."

"I just said I wasn't interested and maybe she had enough to drink. Seemed to work, Burt."

Burt laughed and the shift continued. He told me he was going to see Robbie tomorrow and speak to him about how to treat young women and he would be talking to his mom. His lowlife dad disappeared a while back. Our evening continued without much fuss, the usual banter and laughter resuming as usual until lock up at 12. As I helped clear up, a big fuss descended on the bar. Eve was found outside in a ditch in an awful dead state of affairs. Her abdomen was lying on the road with a rough stick half in and out of her lady parts. Blood, bowel and innards were sprawled all around her. She was definitely dead, but what an awful way to go!

The undertaker was called and he, with help, removed the body from the ditch and the mess off the road. This would be the gossip in the little town about Eve's awful demise for quite a while. Already Burt and Belinda had forgotten about Robbie, as people were suggesting how and what the cause of the death was. For now, gossip would state she had chosen a wrong lay and got what she deserved. However, with the significant torture she had undertaken and the fact that she was no more, opinions would change.

Eve would be remembered fondly in weeks to come; all memories of her being a drunken harlot would dissipate. This tended to happen with death and was always a fascination to me. Humans always had this knack of forgetting the crimes of the now-awfully-slaughtered-to-death person. That night, as I closed the barn door behind me and made my way silently through the town, I thought about Eve. I had whispered in her ear,

"Occidere te inhonoratus es, maximus ad summum donum tuum est enim vita tua. Soli Deo tuo videbimus quomodo divina estis."

It meant: "Kill yourself. You are worthless. Your biggest gift is to end your life. Only your God will see how divine you are."

Awfully stern and meaningful words but the connotation was rhythmic with a Latin strain. It's funny how words said in a foreign language can sound so romantic and sexy. Eve's life was pathetic and worthless, with very little self-respect left. In death, she felt she was gaining respect with her sacrifice to her assailant, the one she had tried to seduce in the bar. She gave herself willingly to him and he desecrated her.

I moved away whilst all the commotion was taking place. No one would even know I had disappeared. I would be back in a flash and no one would ever notice. Slipping away was my speciality and something I was quite proud of.

I approached the front door, blinds drawn and everything quiet. I walked around the property—no sign of anyone. The backdoor was also closed and locked. I crouched until I felt my claws scrape the ground and I extended my wings all the way out to the sides. I raised off the ground and flew up to the second-floor windows. I could see the bathroom and the bedroom. Two adults in bed were asleep. I flew round to the front and spotted him, sitting in bed dozing, eyes closed but not fully asleep. The window was open, a small gap. I squeezed through. Standing in the room at the foot of the bed, I stretched my legs and twisted my neck so I could adapt to my new form. I was a beautiful blonde with long legs and an ample bosom. I imagined roses and the aroma floated under his nose. He sat up and almost screamed, then settled into an almost dreamlike state. I was the image of the girl on his centre pages of his dirty magazine. His desire was strong, making a tent with his dick, as he focussed only on my form. I crept onto the bed and lay beside him, missing all his kisses and avoiding all touches. He was actually mesmerised. I sat astride his puny frame and reached for his throat.

"Why lie to everyone about Lyla?" I said softly.

He stared at me, seeing me for who I really was, and the fear set in. His bladder released and there was a strong smell of faecal matter.

"Oh! Has little Robbie pissed himself? Oh, I see he has shit too! What a big baby!"

Robbie's lack of reaction was to do with his fear. He was paralysed with horror at what he knew was to come.

"I'll make it quick." I reached up and caressed his cheek before snapping his neck.

I then pulled his body out of the bed and decorated his room with his organs. (Best to make it look like an animal attack. Plus, it was fun.) Hearts are loved by everyone, so I stuck his in the window so everyone would appreciate it. I pulled his arms off and wrapped them around the bedside lamp. His legs I sat on the chair with his head in between. His torso was a mess anyway after splitting him from throat to pubic bone. So I left that carcass on the bloodstained bed clothes. I put his penis in his mouth, tool side in so the entrails were hanging out the sides.

So… the little shit eats dick! How that story can be like a virus spreading through town! Lyla will get the last laugh in an ironic way.

My artwork complete, I made my way downstairs. As I walked down each stair, it felt exhilarating knowing I was leaving such an artistic surprise in the child's bedroom. At any moment, anyone could come onto the landing and I would be seen. I probably wouldn't have enough time to change body/form into what would be acceptable... I made myself laugh! What kind of thing would be an acceptable form, for two parents to come face-to-face with, to then try to digest the untimely and dramatic death of their son... I thought possibly an arachnid, not a bird that was too weird. God, I was funny. I decided to slip out the door quietly but leave it unlocked so it would look like a break in of a sort. I left it open with a smashed lock. I actually loved my job!

Part of me wanted to stay with Burt a little longer, but a larger part was pulling me to leave and move onwards on my journey. The journey that governed my destiny, like *déjà vu*, I was reliving each day. So I was living as a non-human, as a dead thing, as no actual heartbeat was a type of boring existence. I had to have some fun, keep myself busy. I had a chuckle. I was leaving town, keeping Burt and Eva's trysts a secret, thus keeping the little family together and happy. Belinda was none the wiser and Burt's secret was safe. On the plus side, Lyla was also safe and all rumours would cease now following Robbie's demise. Fuck me!! I'm a fucking GOD! A legend! A saviour! An Angel!

I decided to leave a letter for Burt and his family to thank them for their kindness and that I hoped they would continue to do well with the business and I would return soon.

Now for a swift exit, I chose my shape, chose my direction, felt the magnetic pull and made like fast food!

Denn die Todten reiten Schnell (for the dead travel fast).

Chapter 6

Not quite sure how long I had been in the air but I had passed through five sunsets that I was aware of. I gained energy from the sun and fuel from the insects and prey I caught as I flew. My wings were strong and my mind set on the end objective. How far away I was now and how many others were also on a path towards it... all unanswered questions. My outer layer felt like leather and I knew I needed to reshape and take a rest.

By the time I felt my feet on the gravel, my claws had unfurled and were replaced with human-shaped feet with boots on. As it was a truck stop, I decided to go for female trucker image. I was dressed for trucking, so not showing anything I shouldn't be and I had a stocky shape but feminine and shapely. I also had extraordinarily long, brown, silky hair which I wore in a bun on the top of my head, with silver stud earrings, thick silver chain at my neck and a solid silver watch. I was independent, feminine, strong, capable and independent. Unbeknown to everyone, I didn't have a truck with me, but I intended to remedy that pretty quickly.

As the sun rose, I felt quite small in comparison to the beautiful glow approaching us. I looked around the car park; there were five large tanker trucks, three rigids and a pickup truck which looked extremely minute like a tonka toy sat next to real trucks. The vehicles were very impressive like extraterrestrial beings just waiting for the moment to launch themselves onto their prey. At the time I appeared in the car park, the drivers were up and getting ready for their day, some eating breakfast, some in the cab still making preparations. One of the rigids drove past me with a burly man behind the wheel. He pipped the horn to signal bye to whoever. The flat terrain had seconds to prepare for the hefty truck with 14 wheels to rain upon it, taking roadkill like confetti, pulverising and chucking to the side of the road, a beast with no scruples or regrets upon a normal, quiet, passive roadway.

King of the road came to mind. This mechanical beast didn't care if you were small, fat, tall, thin, white, black, mammal or reptilian. If you got in the way of these tyres, you were squashed. It actually fascinated me how a small compact shape could spread out so far across tarmac like pate on toast. There was no escape under those wheels.

In the time it took me to walk to the door, three more vehicles had entered and one tanker had left. Today was a busy day. I wasn't fanatical over colour, but I was impressed with size and I was keen to take in the view of the larger trucks. I especially liked the tankards which, I learnt through observation, carried liquid, most of this flammable. With the signs along the side stating hazardous material, it was easy to guess. This excited me as the thought of being in charge of a dangerous vehicle was risky, especially if you encountered a maniac or a serial killer. I watched as a Class Two rigid pulled on with a curtain sider. This was approximately 30 feet in length. This vehicle you would not argue with. This info I found out minutes later drinking strong tea and eating a hearty breakfast with my fellow road riders, the endless interesting chat with what loads we had and where we were going, issues with hitchhikers, police checks, usual stuff…

My food was wet, soggy and almost slimy. It was tasty. There was no denying that. Flavours were strong together, but individually it all tasted of fat. Fried bread (in my opinion) is the biggest factor towards a human heart disease. If I had had a heart, it would have been begging me to stop feeding myself with so much grease, but, I didn't have a heart of the usual description or I would have walked past this stop and left all these working people alone. I watched a bloke take a mouthful of his sausage sandwich, and while he chewed on it, the fat dribbled down the sides of his mouth and over his chin onto his top where it congealed with yesterday's menus. A bit of sausage threatened to run out of his mouth, and he used his index finger to shove that greasy motherfucker back into the death tunnel. He was already preparing for the next bite whilst chatting with his mate who was very thin and seemed to be piling it all in, desperate to put some weight on! He had a triple special. This was a bacon, sausage and egg sandwich. He must have asked for it with extra fat!! The poor bread was limp in his hands, almost apologising to him about not being able to hold the filling in place. That's all bread had to do. The job seemed easy, stay on the outside hold the filling in place. "We are to be eaten." The poor slices had had every chance taken away from them. Limp with fat, all they could do was lie back and watch it all go to shit. However, the men just sank their greedy teeth into it all, letting the fat congeal around their molars and spurt out the sides as they talked to each other. They sent smiles my way, which was like a comedy/horror show for the tickled stomachs. They were chewing with open mouths, pools of fat hanging off chins, some of the sauce and breakfast juices up their noses and wearing the evidence of meal choices from previous days. Plus, the food got caught in the teeth, waving at me! These men were a sure catch for someone!

As the morning passed, the place filled up, and a steady stream of truckers drove in and drove out. I decided I was there for the night. I commandeered a truck, an articulated lorry with a 45-foot trailer. The trailer had a mechanical sheeting over the top to protect the load. This was worked via the fob in the cab. The cab was spacious with a double bed behind the driver and passenger seats. The load I was carrying was full of coal. Coal had a particular smell, an earthy metallic smell and a nice hard feel to it. My cab was warm and spacious. I had plenty of food packed away in the cupboards above the steering wheel and behind my head above the bed. The inside was nice, really nice. I could almost call it home apart from the still-bleeding Harold squashed in the foot well with a blanket on top of him. God, he's a bleeder! And a moaner!

"Just die already, will you!? You have no stomach contents, nothing to live for, so die! And try and do it quieter."

I got a moan in reply but with less vigour to it. He was on his way out. Thank God! I could have ended it sooner. I could have gone for the heart, and straight away he would have gone but for some reason, I wanted it slow. I had acquiesced to a drink in the cab and this was his undoing. After seeing his tool, slicing it off his body and then inserting my long index-finger nail into the gaping hole and slicing from right to left and then up and down, allowing the inners to fall out, I then pushed him into the footwell, pressing hard on his back and head until I heard some inaudible cracks. I threw the blanket over his head as a comfort thing. I had some heart, sort of.

I shook the blood off me completely. I wasn't even tempted to lick any of it or chew on any innards, as the amount of fat I had already consumed was enough, without me consuming any further from a fat-induced dying Harold. He was too far into his death throes for me to be successful in scaring him to be quiet, so I turned on the radio. To my delight, it was *The Vogues* with *Turn Around; Look at Me.* Those lyrics were so apt for our situation.

"There is someone walking behind you. Turn around; look at me.

There is someone watching your footsteps. Turn around; look at me."

Yep, he should have really been on the ball, seen me coming, turned around and got a proper look at the monster I really am. Poor old Harold! He came and he stuffed his fat gut and he didn't look properly around him. I listened as he took his last gargled, troubled breaths. He was now in the land of the deceased to then face whatever had in store for him there.

And now I'm left with a fat slob of a body. Maybe I will find a use for him.

I checked my load and, in doing so, noticed how closely packed the coal was and the smell and the touch was magnificently smooth and cold. I checked the sheeting; it was powered by a machine in the cab. The gap between the cab and the trailer was sufficient to stand and see how the whole contraption worked.

"So what you packing?" a gruff voice asked me.

I had actually forgot I was a female and silently cursed for not shifting.

"Coal, where you parked?"

"I'm the gas truck, sweet pea, and I'm carrying a huge load of gas!!" His drawling accent was hideous. He was so desperate for a chat up line that he was using the size of his vehicle to impress little ole me!

I covered up my distaste and presented an overconfident smile. "Well, size does matter. My name's Beverley. You can call me Bev."

"I'm Big Lee, and you can call me anything you want, sugar," he drawled and dribbled. We arranged to get a drink and I said I would meet him at the café, just needed to recheck my load. Where I was positioned, I was overlooked the one side very well indeed and at the front. I used my cloaking device to shield me from carrying the body out of the cab and shoving it under the coal in the trailer. This was a tricky performance and I had to balance the mechanical sheeting, along with the levity of coal and the corpse, as well as keeping it all behind the naked eye. The level of concentration needed to do this was immense. I was a high-ranking levitation realm wicker, so I was blessed a little. Gifts like this made life easier for me.

I entered the café in my female fatale form and received some stares and nods from customers sitting around. The all-consuming fat-cooking smells took over me again, making me nauseous and heady. I headed for the counter to get some strong coffee, anything to distract me from the pungent aroma. I talked a lot of general rubbish, enough to up my façade and satisfy curiosity, keeping people at arm's length. I saw Lee signalling me from his table. He had two other truckers with him, both engrossed in their conversation. As I got to the spare seat, they all looked up and the two other men smiled before continuing their conversation. Lee and I chatted general stuff, veering into home life and social activities. Lee was a married man with three kids all over the age of 15 years. He was separated from his wife and had been living the single life now for about six years. He saw his kids still every other weekend if he wasn't on the road. He got on with his wife a lot better now since they parted and she had moved on and got herself a new boyfriend. Lee appeared OK with this but wasn't keen on the co-parenting thing.

I was comfortable chatting rubbish with him; it felt good and his flirty brashness had disappeared. Humans always amazed me; they had a purpose in life to appear in an expected form or way in front of others, to behave in a way that cloaked them, made them appear acceptable or appealing. It certainly helped beings like myself hopping in and out of realms to do it undiscovered and unsuspected, as we could also adapt using these cloaks that humans regularly used as a way of existing. Lee's cloak was one of macho, womanising and a wise cracking fool. This, in his opinion, gave him an edge to pick up women and also be a great man's drinking buddy. He had a good personality and this was highlighted as we chatted.

As we looked around the café, it was full to brimming with chatty, jolly workers, all trying to usurp the other but in a light way, nothing serious or malicious. The showers at the back were very busy with a constant flow of users and a smell of aromatic shampoos and aftershave. Lee said he was off to use the shower and he said he would see me after. I watched him go and eyed up my meals. There was no shortage of ready meals at my fingertips, and I had to choose wisely. My aperitif was making his way back to his cab. Around middle 50s with a stout frame and approximately six feet, he walked with a slight limp. I watched him make his way out the café and towards the car park. I tried to guess which truck he would get into, but I was wrong. He walked in a diagonal trajectory towards a long vehicle but, at the last minute, turned left towards a camper vehicle. This vehicle was not actually seen unless you walked past the truck. As I neared the camper, I heard muffled whispers and giggling followed by moans. The passion in the air was thick and hid my tentative approach. I stood at the door, taking in my surroundings—quiet and private (due to the angle of the truck). I dissolved my form into mist and pushed under the door of the van. As I got half my form back, appearing as a man, wearing a dark hooded cloak, I was aware a man on his hands and knees noticed my arrival. He tensed up and screamed shrilly (possibly due to my bottom end being moulded into the front driver's seat. My 50-year-old seemed in pain, trying to remove himself from the anal area of the younger man. As I stepped forward, climbing further into the vehicle, I forced my fist into the throat area, pulling out the tongue and bottom jaw, successfully shutting the screaming man up. I lazily dropped these on the floor of the vehicle and, with my dry hand, grabbed my victim around the throat. As I pulled his head up, he became detached from the younger man and gave himself to me without any resistance. I got from his aura that this was him feeling he was being punished from engaging in same sex, which he appeared to have a confused reaction to. I bit into his head, sucking on his brains and ripping out his jugular vein with my free hand, enjoying the fresh flow over my body. I made it quick, drinking all fluid offered. The brains were old and a bit chewy but edible. His limp penis was pitiful but obviously offered some satisfaction to the guy jawless on the floor. He was in a state of shock and rolling around jawless. I put him out of his misery by stomping full on his head. This took two full stomps, as I was careful the first time and wanted to see how much pain he could take. After draining his corpse of blood and eating his heart whole, I looked over my feast. God, that was some buffet aperitif. Now for the tidy up and then onto Lee…

It took me longer than I thought and I didn't want to use my mage to sort my mess out. It always took so much energy from me and I had to recuperate. After cleaning body debris into realm bags, I tidied round and left the van looking neater than it was when I materialised. Leaving the same way I entered, I continued on my route to my truck. With my bag of body debris in the realm, I again shoved body pieces in amongst the coal. Some pieces fell out and a man walked past, getting closer to see what the noise was. I stayed where I was suspended in the realm and I hovered invisibly above his head. As the security light went off again and the sound of muffled chatter from the café filled the air, I fell down onto his back, sinking my teeth into his head right through to brain matter. Sucking and chewing, I effectively drained him like a prune reducing his body to an insignificant piece of dried up flesh. I folded him up in half and shoved him into the gap between the cab and the flatbed part. With his bones all cracking as I folded him, it made me think of the bubble wrap I had seen kids pop. At least with him so stuffed in, he didn't resemble anything now. He was just an indiscernible small mass of something.

As I stood up, I sensed a familiar smell... Lee. I shifted into my female form and hovered around the front of the cab, looking like I was checking the tyres. He strolled up to me, reverting back to Mr Charmy Pants with a bolshy attitude. That was his real undoing, as I had got to like him and may have possibly left him alone. After some heated sexual intercourse, he was lying back in the bed having a smoke and smiling at me.

"You sure you don't mind me smoking in here?" he asked me smugly.

"I'm OK with my food smoked, adds to the flavour..." I calmly crooned into his ear before tracing my tongue down his neck to his chest, down to his belly button and then swooping back up to his chest area. My tongue had sensitive receptor points on it, so it absorbed feeling and produced tension and excitement. Lee had another erection, and as he moaned loudly, I held onto his tool with my one hand, getting a rhythm going. I continued to lick up his chest where I hovered above the top of the sternum. When Lee was about to ejaculate, I sank my whole face into his chest, opening skin, cracking tough sternum bone and continuing down until I got a mouthful of lung. Moving over slightly, I chomped on his heart. Feeling his life source leave his body in as much of a rush as his semen did was one of the most thrilling moments.

I placed Lee carefully in the coal again with my other conquest. I was feeling such a rush of emotions and power and I flew across to the café, pushing the door through smashing the windows. As the glass was falling onto the floor and the customers still in shock trying to work out what was happening, I took a person at a time, swiftly biting, slicing and ripping them apart. I left entrails in my wake as I moved across to each person. My mess at the end of it all was epic. It looked like a bloodbath—slippery, slimy mess all around formed out of body parts. I had eaten enough to last me into the forever and beyond. Walking was treacherous, and I knew I was placing myself at risk of twisting an ankle and slipping on everything. This I was not prepared to clean up. I exited the building and brought down two more truckers just about to enter. Getting slower due to so much buffet, I decided a plan had to be put into action.

I made my way outside and started up one of the tankers. I drove out of the car park and down the road. Turning around in the nearest layby, I set myself up for impact. Gathering some speed, I put my foot down and headed straight, careering into the petrol pumps and then the café. I exited the truck in the midst of the bangs and the flames. The noise on impact shook the world around it and the impending storm of other impacts was just as startling. I walked through the chaos, the flames licking my long black coat and catching my black hair, highlighting the silvery glow and dripping off onto the flammable surface of the road. Oh, beautiful fire, beautiful heat! Gas pumps exploding, café lighting up, trucks being caught in it, other tankers being close enough to tag them with the heat, flames and falling debris. A bonfire of such magnitude, an expression of joy, a celebration of my meal, and a fitting mass cremation of my unconsumed food.

A beacon of light for humans to be curious of, and challenge gossip around the event, a siren for others to know something had taken place and revel at the possibilities of what.

It was time to continue with my walk...

"We can't underestimate the value of silence. We need to create ourselves. Need to spend time alone. If you don't, you risk not knowing yourself and not realising your dreams."
quotefancy.com/quote/1257572

Chapter 7

The feeling of floating in and out of realms was so wonderful, but I knew I had to be careful. I could dip in there and not come out, so extra care had to be used to maintain constant vigilance. Onward and upwards was the saying, onwards with the walk to my goal.

Distance travelled in and out the parallels, cannot be measured and its links to each side can affect the weather. Sometimes, the crackle of thunder or a burst of lightning can signal an entity from one realm, pushing through the curtain of difference. To humans, this is mere weather changes but to outsiders, this is a warning that we are not alone, the many types of being, crossing over to escape from persecution or to travel from one place to another. Recent changes to the realms with leadership and rebirths led to curiosity too. This can only be quenched by being in the physical.

My magnetic feeling was back, along with a pull for information. I had cut across realms, interrupted time and shot backwards and forwards in my quest to find more information. The secrets I needed, the wholesome feeling I desired, would be soon fulfilled. My continuous road was endless, and my victims were increasing in number each time I stopped. My truck stop adventure was phenomenal, but I was alerting others to my existence. At the time, I really didn't care, as I was sated and that took priority.

I had been in many a fight, with my kind and similar. With human kind, this was no fight; this was a tussle mostly emotional and verbal. Weapons slowed me down but did not kill me, so a fight with normal beings was sometimes frustrating but fun. With subnormal, it was a thrill and a genuine fight to survive. I needed some of that, I felt, as it was so easy to become complacent. As if I had wished it, I was thrown to the side and with a flash of light pulled backwards. Damn it! I was daydreaming, I lost control and my senses failed to detect an Arcato. This was a canine type of creature with a giant head and protruding jaw. Long doglike torso with four legs, it was always in a pack—never alone—and never had a satisfied appetite. I knew I was in a spot of bother and I had to be quick but purposefully attacking. In this situation with an Arcato, defence was not an element of choice to survive but aggression and killing was. An Arcato could not comprehend submission but had to be destroyed. It may be led by the pack and placed into tiers of aggressiveness, thus gaining power but the sole reason for survival, was pack domination, survival and unquenched satisfaction.

I smiled and showed my front line of teeth. The being jumped around me, lashing out with his long claws and snapping its huge jaws as it did an about turn, to come back to me for slashing again. This one was a different version; it was toying with me, playing with its food. The pack retreated, watching it pan out. Word was that I was food, so enjoy the fight. I lowered myself to the ground in a cowering position, allowing it to feel it could take its time to approach. As I lay with my head down, back bent over to the floor, my limbs in the male humanoid form pulled in underneath my torso and the Arcato came in for the kill. It sank its claws into the spine, which I had jellified to take the actual assault, and as I allowed my spine to contract at the cervical point, I detached my head from the neck, keeping it together with a jellified substance and I opened my frontal jaws and allowed my two sets behind to protrude and take a hold of the neck of the beast. As I crunched down, the front set of teeth sank in, twisting and turning until the whole head came loose from the torso. I stood up, taking on the Arcato form for the top half of my body and throwing the severed head at the feet of the pack. On my humanoid legs, I stretched out my spine and transformed again, this time into a dragon-type creature with a scorpion tail. The pack backed off in one fluid movement and a light opened up to my right where I shot through with ease. Landing onto firmer terrain, I got myself into a humanoid male form again.

"Oh hey! You OK? Where did you appear from?" sweet and innocent was the voice and the subject was a girl with long, dark plaits.

"Uhm, I have this habit of appearing out of nowhere. Sorry if I startled you." I put my head down realising I had morphed into a young boy about 11. I was always amazed with myself how I just knew how to morph into what would suit the surroundings. I was back on firmer territory breathing in oxygenated air.

"Let's play," and off she ran with me in her slip stream.

I acclimatised quickly to my new form and surroundings. Subconsciously checking my clothes, I glanced around. At the play area, there was a small roundabout with a soft tarmac surrounding, a larger roundabout with a swing set, accommodating all ages and a few different slides going into sand. At the back was a maze of apparatus including climbing walls, castle-like buildings to hide in and create imaginative play and a water park with fountains on concrete areas and false ducks on a small pretend lake.

In a small child format, I was conscious of being too mature and giving reactions too quick so I slowed down to be more infantile. I mimicked other children's behaviour and actions to gain a reasonable accepted appearance. The girl was a fast runner and way more athletic than what you would think at first sight. She had an ability to manipulate people around her, making herself look good, sweet but getting her own way. And this was at the age of 10!! Serial killer in the making here…

We ducked and dived, racing through small people and darting around big people. We giggled, shouted, screamed and just made inaudible squeals as we continued on our journey. She made people angry. Then they saw her sweet face and smiled. She was like some sort of mood-changing, controlling-mind worker. Then it came to me like a blast. She's an influencer!! She was definitely human in form but a talented uprising influencer, capable of encouraging people to make decisions based on what they feel were their choices. In fact, these were only what she wanted them to do. It worked like a spell to blind some people from the facts but always to benefit the spellbinder. My little Witchling appeared oblivious to her powers and manipulation and continued on with her play. My time here was supposed to be short but children were so much fun, and who can blame me for a little light relief? By the time we had worn ourselves out for an hour, I heard the raised voices.

"Elizabeth!!!!" the shrill voice said. This sounded caring as well as determined.

Elizabeth grinned at me. "See you tomorrow," she said as she ran to her mother.

This was an order, a direct one but again said with a flippancy to the tone. She knew I would be back tomorrow. I sat on the roundabout, watching as children were claimed and taken away on their journey home. No one looked at me with interest. No one asked why I was there and who my parents were. This isn't because no one cared; it was because everyone was running busy lives with time, I may have events, routines to follow, lives to live. I did think I may have to cloak myself, going invisible to divert attention elsewhere. However, here in this childlike form, I was safe for now.

As the park emptied and the vacant space became more obvious, I decided to use my cloaking technique and I faded into the shadows.

I had no idea how many days I had spent by the park and the amount of friends I had made as each day merged into another. Strange how you can be everywhere and nowhere at the same time. No questions asked, no worried looks or concern shown due to me not having an adult at my side. The world had suddenly become dependent on media and texting, social messaging and opinions shared. As long as the kids were deposited at the play area, the necessary commenting via devices began. This was accompanied with verbal gossiping amongst individual; carefully sought out groups. Occasionally, a woman would raise her head to see if her kid was visible and once ascertained, the head would turn to listen to the ongoing conversation or tilt downwards to return to online messaging.

I gathered from the very loud talk that a like was as significant as a comment. The simple task of pressing like could be interpreted in so many different ways. Scenarios were then given to add to the action, thus making the effect of the LIKE action much more meaningful whether it be in a negative or positive way. This cluck of women was almost territorial in the daily way they met and how their behaviour signalled their animosity towards others outside of their circle; whether this was virtual or in the flesh real time. They were like parasites living off the virtual world feel and the effects they craved.

The children were left to be children and they really were scarily left. As long as visible at times of looking up, all was fine with the world. I got the feeling that the children felt like products, but instead of being on a shelf, they were left to get rid of the pent up energy and then return to robot lives until the same time tomorrow.

There was a mirrored element with the children but it was not as obvious as the adults. No child was ostracised but there was a pecking order. This was seen when they lined up for the slide or they chose a swing. Dependent on what swing they chose depicted on where they stood on that day in favour of overall popularity. I was the new kid but the one that wasn't known, so I was indispensable, unnoticeable, unpopular but not enough to be discarded.

No one asked me about my mom. No one asked what school I went to or where I lived. Maybe that would come in time (which, of course, I was running short of). It was good to play, run around, climb and get into so many tiny heads and overworked minds. The youthful energy coming off these children was intoxicating. I was inhaling it to almost suck the youthfulness out, consuming it myself. In comparison, the 'mothers' were quite bitter and there was a falseness surrounding them. It felt a bit like aspartame, used as a sweetener replacement for sugar. There was an acceptance but an all-time knowing it wasn't the same.

Day in, day out, I got to know my buffet. Sweet and sour it would be and I would need to choose my moment.

Killing day came and went quite swiftly—the best yet. The soft flesh, the tender bones cracking under my grip, the sweet flow of innocent life blood and the begging, pleading looks and squeals for help would be a part of my favourite repertoire to play and replay at my desire, the shock when I started to crawl up the steep slide and I opened my vast mouth like a cave to catch the first three kids as they slid down towards me, having no hope in hell of stopping or changing direction. As I crunched on the bones and wiped the blood off my chin, I remained in the child form, as I felt this helped to offer more reason to create fear.

As I mounted the slide, I had already snatched two more kids who I tore apart from the one shoulder all the way down to the groin. I threw them to the ground, knowing a clean-up job would be a sweet for me. As I stood looking down surveying my prey, I noticed parents were moving, phones cast aside and moving towards their fledglings to save them.

Huh! Like they actually cared! I had been around a few weeks and no one asked who I was and questioned my intentions. But now that lives had been taken, they suddenly cared??? False prophets. I tore down on them like a missile, ripping them limb from limb, decapitating heads and tearing legs off the torsos, watching them still trying to cling onto life and crawl away. I twisted heads till they were facing the wrong way and I shoved heads up bottoms. God, these were such an arse licker, a brown noser! What a way to die! Suffocated in their false heroes' inners!

The children stopped screaming and running and stood still. The mothers left alive but in pieces on the floor sobbed strangely awkward bursts. One said to me, "Why?"

I crouched by her and held her head in my lap and stroked her hair, watching the blood congeal around her torn off leg. I shoved my hand up the gap in the torn flesh and kept going until it reached the intestines.

"Because I can," I whispered softly as I tore out the innards. She died there and then in my arms, how sweet the look in her eyes was as she realised I didn't care and how there was no mercy left for her or anyone. I gouged out her right eyeball with my index finger, severing the tendon at the back as it came out with a resounding plop. It had already started to glaze over but still tasted fresh and alive as I bit through the clear vitreous jellylike substance. This was much more fluid like the older owner of the eye. I was looking forward to sucking the firm jelly out of the fledgling's eyes. I stood up straight, sucking the juices from under my finger nails.

The children stood whimpering and when I looked up at them, raising both arms in the air, they lined up. As I surveyed my table offerings, I noticed movement to my left. There was life in the tunnel. I swept my eyes over the line of bodies and they all sat down together on the floor in a defeated stance to await their fate.

I quietly and swiftly made my way to the playground. I stood at the side of the tunnel, listening to the breathing and feeling the tense nervousness of the human the other side of the concrete. I decided to play it slow and calm. No need to rush at this thing. I floated above the tunnel in my childlike form, waiting. The hushed sounds, I was delighted to find came from two forms. The whispering was getting intense with one sound becoming firmer.

Aww! People, we have a genuine hero in our midst. He is going to come out and check the area to see if it's safe while the pathetic weakling stays inside.

"Come out. Come out from where you are," I whispered. The movement stopped suddenly. I could just reach in and pull one out but I liked the chase and the fear factor. I smelt the piss very strongly and wondered which one had emptied their bladder, or maybe both. The thing with fear was that it was quite contagious. Bitter, bitter fear but resulting in sweet meat. Petrified meat on my victims was much more sweet and tasty. I knew I would not be able to keep drawing this out for much longer. The feeling was getting too much for me. I felt I would burst.

As a few moments went on, one child came crawling out and started to run fast into the woods at the side of the park. I let him go. I would catch him later. Within around five minutes, a tubby little boy came through the opening and carefully looked around and up. He met my cold stare. He lost his bladder again and the stench was full-on strong. He didn't run or turn, just stood, still never breaking the stare. I rose above him, making my body vertical like an arrow with me pointing up to the sky. I lowered myself down towards him slowly, opening my mouth wide at the last minute, consuming him from head to toe. As I stood on firmer ground, straightening up, I had his shoes sticking out of my mouth. I flicked them off and sucked the feet in at the last minute. I gulped like a snake just holding it all in. It would atrophy and I would benefit from the added vitamins and the feast itself. He was a mouthful indeed. I looked around the area and saw the remains of my buffet with the adults. Ha! What a bloody mess, entrails everywhere and blood and gore akimbo.

The sun shone down on the putrefied mess, lighting it up even more. The blood/fluid was leaking into the earth and the nearby drains. The carcasses were left over scraps for me and I summoned the rats into the area to help me dispose of the remains. Hearing them chomping and chewing was music to my ears. The slurping of the baby rats made me smile. What a genuine good deed I was doing! Bless my socks! Let the babies live well and full.

I snapped out of my idling mood when I heard scampering and heavy breaths, alerting me to my escapee making his way through the woods. This woodland was thick and full of fallen down branches and foxholes. The terrain was bumpy and difficult for two feet and I had every confidence I could stop him before he reached the perimeter of the wood and managed to signal attention. I shifted into a wolf form and tore off at a sprint. As he saw me approach, he shouted and screamed and I neatly bit into his neck, tearing the head from his body. I didn't have the heart to continue with his suffering. I was such a good soul.

After throwing his head and torso up into the nearest tree, I sprinted back to my children. They were just finishing off the carcasses and they were dragging them down the drains into the sewers. My human children were sat in the line heads down, all looking robotic. I summoned them to stand up and, still in my wolf form, asked them who they would invite to a party. The consensus was a clown. I changed my form to a very large colourful clown and I enveloped each child at a time. I bit, chewed and sucked at each child and I took my time to devour each part of every one. Being young and supple, I was able to enjoy the sweet meat and suck on the underdeveloped brains, draining the life force out of every single child. Willingly, they gave themselves up to me. Willingly, they sacrificed their life blood and their childlike souls.

The dome I had created over the park area to camouflage the damage I had delivered was slowly fading. I let it fade and I shifted back to my child form to make my way out of the park area. I walked away, head held high, and I passed people making their way to work, on their way to meet friends for social meets, etc. As I disappeared into the fog, I heard the imminent screams as bodies and debris were found and police were called. My handywork would be discussed for years to come.

I went again on my long, long walk. I was always alone in my quest and these drop-offs were an escape to get some company, but to inevitably be me. It would be nice that I often thought to be with someone or something, to be around some life, to be liked, loved, wanted and looked up to. I often made a flamboyant wish.

Walk on, walk onnnnnnnn, with hope in your heart,
And you'll never walk alone.
You'll never walk alone…

Oscar Hammertsein11/Richard rogers.

Deep, dark night, oh, heavenly laden with death awaits me. Remains of some form of life from before and after littering the land, underneath and miles down. Rising out of the earth stood an object looking like a thick spear but in fact was joined at the trunk to an old hand-fashioned out of stone. The magnetic pull was intangible and devouring. All of my journey and time had been for this sweet moment. As I wrapped my hand around that hand, I shifted from form to form at the speed of light and my body rippled between each one, giving me pleasure upon pleasure combined with an electricity which tore up the surrounding areas.

My destiny was to be unfolded and my path of manipulation and destruction would be supported by many followers. My name would be Jesus, and I would be known to many to heal wounds and amend afflictions, to create history and amass a huge following. I would be so powerful. I would be able to rule a country at a time and then the world. I would be known by many different names but honoured and in awe of everyone. I was aware a shift in the realm would begin, alerting all species of my success and their ultimate submission. I had been drawn to this place, this spot, and I was the first to succeed.

During my reign, I would continue to exist when my body would be used as crucifixion to attempt to remove power. I would always continue to live, both the good and evil in the same body and existing between realms. Supporters would embrace the fact that good people would be rewarded with a thought, feeling, sometimes a dream or a vision. They would accept and embrace punishments handed out to those opposed to the belief. The firmer the punishments, the best the lessons learnt. The evil that men do can sometimes be an order and the act not representing the heinous delivery, but the order being carried out. What goes around comes around.

I am able to mask in many religions and beliefs and when it becomes all too much of a boring ride, I can always create an earth shattering, ground-breaking physical tragedy, thus sending out a message, regain followers and reinforce a belief. If I felt we were becoming overrun, I can chuck in a virus to wipe a few million out. This always rewarded me with a sustainable following and desperation for life to return as what once was always came with new followers.

Cults, satanic groups and communes would continue to grow and provide me with my own hell on an earth plain. It was always so wonderful to be both God and Satan in the same cloth. This was my destiny, my whole plan, and I had delivered.

Be careful who and what you pray to. For thine IS the kingdom, the power and the glory forever and ever.
Amen…

Made in the USA
Monee, IL
03 May 2026